Z Is for Zombie

WRITTEN BY Merrily Kutner

ILLUSTRATED BY John Manders

ALBERT WHITMAN & COMPANY

MORTON GROVE, ILLINOIS

For my son, Jonathan,

and because of him.

— M. K.

For Donna.

— J. M.

Library of Congress Cataloging-in-Publication Data

Kutner, Merrily.
Z is for zombie / by Merrily Kutner ; illustrated by John Manders.
p. cm.

Summary:
Illustrations and rhyming text present a night full of scary creatures
and spooky sights, one for each letter of the alphabet.
ISBN 0-8075-9490-3
[1. Halloween—Fiction. 2. Stories in rhyme. 3. Alphabet.]
I. Manders, John, ill.   II. Title.
PZ8.3.K965Zae   1999
[E]—DC21   99-17839
CIP

The illustrations are rendered in watercolor and gouache.
The display type is set in Moonshine Murky.
The text type is set in Manticore.
The design is by Scott Piehl.

Alien

Alien beings without a face
land in ships from outer space.

Bogeyman

Darkness masks the Bogeyman
till you're sleeping—that's his plan.

Cyclops

One-eyed ogre hides away—
Cyclops seizes all who stray.

Dracula

Dracula rises in the night,
searching for a neck to bite.

Eyeball

Eyeballs lined up by the sink
stare from jars without a blink.

Frankenstein's Monster

Lightning bolts at half-past nine
jolt the freak of Frankenstein!

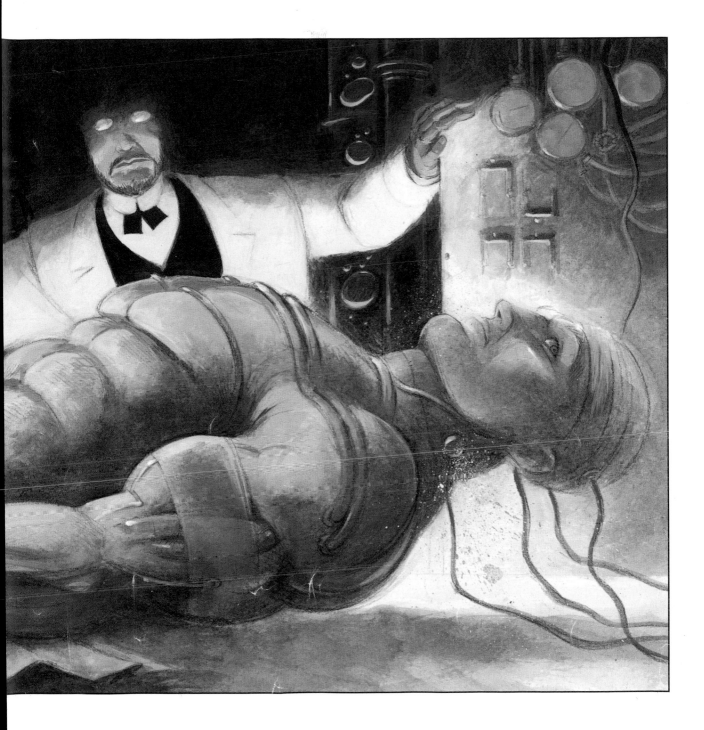

Ghost

An eerie figure haunts the stair.
You peek again—but no one's there.

Haunted House

A crumbling mansion on the hill—
screams and moans are echoing still.

Imp

The Imp must serve the wizard well,
and help him cast his evil spell.

Jack-O'-Lantern

Hideous pumpkin's wicked grin
glares from flickering light within.

Knight

Cloaked in metal, armed to fight,
rides a horseman—the Black Knight.

Loch Ness Monster

Is it legend? Is it real?
The Loch Ness Monster won't reveal.

Mummy

A rotting smell seeps in the room
as Mummies stagger from their tomb.

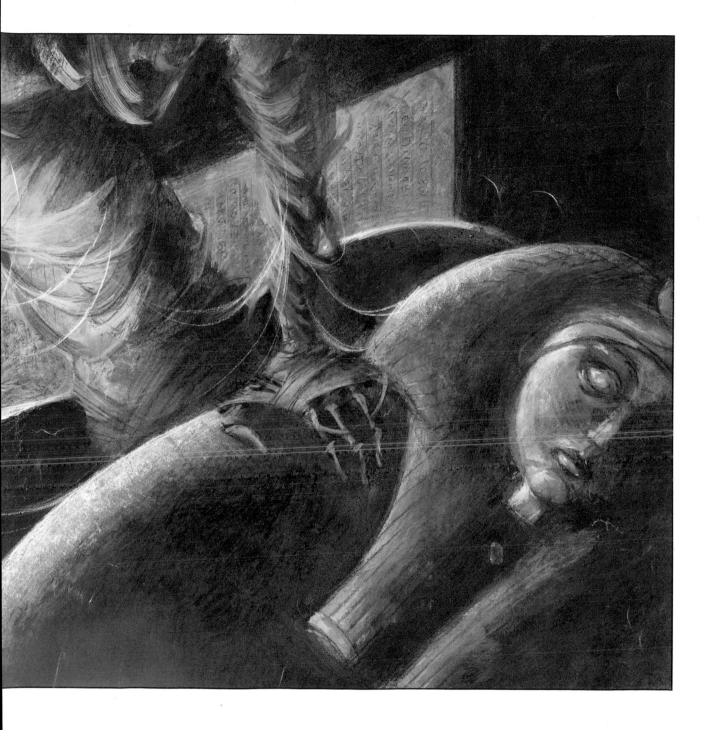

Nightstalker

Hides in shadow, sleeps by day—
grabs its catch and darts away.

Ooze

Greenish Ooze creeps 'neath the door,
bubbling there along the floor.

Poltergeist

As pictures shatter off the wall
a torso floats beyond the hall.

Queen

You see the Queen, but where's her head?
She holds it in her hands instead!

Robot

Programmed circuits, sensors keen—
who commands this crazed machine?

Skeleton

Skeletons rattle 'round your bed—
bony fingers poke your head!

Tarantula

Hairy brown Tarantulas crawl
in your room…and up your wall…

UFO

Menacing ships light up the skies.
Invasion Earth intensifies!

Viper

Serpents strike without delay—
fangs with venom pierce their prey.

Werewolf

Beneath the moon a Werewolf howls.
Transformed by night, he slyly prowls.

X

X marks the spot—an open grave.
A coffin lies as shadows wave.

Yeti

On mountaintop, amid the snow,
looms the Yeti—friend or foe?

Zombie

From the earth the Zombies rise.
Walking corpses terrorize!

Beware the night and what it brings…
for out there lurk such scary things!